Baby Bear
goes to the ZOO

Lorette Broekstra

BRIMAX

For Emma and Ruben

First published in Great Britain in 2000 by Brimax
an imprint of Octopus Publishing Group Ltd
2-4 Heron Quays, London E14 4JP
UK, North American and South African licencee © Octopus Publishing Group Ltd
Text and illustrations © Lorette Broekstra 1999
Originally published in Australia 1999 by Thomas C. Lothian Pty Ltd
Isbn 1858541913
Printed in Italy

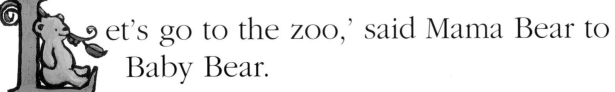 et's go to the zoo,' said Mama Bear to Baby Bear.

They quickly packed a picnic lunch
and set off for the zoo.

They decided to visit the giraffe first.
'Look at his lovely long neck,' said Mama Bear.

'What's that?' asked Baby Bear,
brushing his ear with his paw.
'It's a butterfly!' said Mama Bear.

Just then the butterfly fluttered away.
Baby Bear scampered after it.

He chased the butterfly past the elephants,

past the lions,

past the zebras,

and past the monkeys,
until the butterfly disappeared over a wall.

Poor Baby Bear was all alone!
He began to cry, but then he heard,
'Baby Bear! Baby Bear!'

Baby Bear ran to see who was calling him.

'You're not my mama!' said Baby Bear,
'Why are you calling me?'
'I'm Mama Panda Bear and I'm calling
my baby for lunch.'

'Oh!' said Baby Bear sadly,
and he set off to find his mama.
He hadn't gone very far before he heard,

'Baby Bear! Baby Bear!'

Baby Bear ran to see who was calling him.

'You're not my mama!' said Baby Bear,
'Why are you calling me?'
'I'm Mama Brown Bear and I'm calling
my baby for lunch.'

'Oh!' said Baby Bear disappointedly,
and he set off to find his mama.
He hadn't gone very far before he heard,

'Baby Bear! Baby Bear!'

Baby Bear ran to see who was calling him.

'You're not my mama!' said Baby Bear,
'Why are you calling me?'
'I'm Mama Polar Bear and I'm calling
my baby for lunch.'

'Oh!' said Baby Bear helplessly,
and he set off to find his mama.
He hadn't gone very far before he heard,

'Baby Bear! Baby Bear!'
'There you are Baby Bear! I've found you!'

It was Mama!

Baby Bear ran all the way

to meet his mama.

'Where have you been?' asked Mama Bear.
'It's lunchtime!'
'I know,' said Baby Bear.